THE ALIEN'S VOYAGE

GRACE KENSINGTON

1

———

Ivy glanced up as Maxim approached her, offering him a smile. She felt the relief flow through her knowing that she could look at him, reach out and touch him, and know that he was safe even among the Denynso warriors who had just recently been completely set on killing him. She wondered if she was ever going to get over that sense of relief, and just being close to the man who she had fallen so deeply in love with without having to worry that any moment he would be dragged out of her arms again. Even if she didn't ever get over that feeling, she knew that she would always appreciate that she had the ability to feel it, that she hadn't lost him in the dark, terrifying moments that she was positive Pyra would simply destroy the entire group of Mikana men who had come to the Nyx 23 settlement.

Her eyes drifted from Maxim to Pyra as he entered the hall. He looked tired and drawn and Ivy could only imagine that Eden had sent him out of the house to come join the revelry so that he could get a break from their new baby. Having only been around babies of any kind when he was extremely young and the other warriors were born, Pyra seemed to be taken aback by the realities of the tiny, needy creature who was at once the most beautiful and beloved thing that he had ever seen, and the most terrifying, by his own admission. Eden had stepped into motherhood with much greater ease and confidence than Pyra had stepped into fatherhood, and though he was completely in love with his newborn son and was as prepared as he was when they were on their quest to protect Lysander from anything, Ivy could see on his face that taking a break and returning to the world that he already knew and was comfortable in would do him good.

As she watched the leader of the Denynso warriors walk through the banquet hall and drop down onto the bench of one of the long tables and reach for a piece of bread, she couldn't help but still feel a touch of animosity toward him. She wished that she didn't and that she had the ability to shove the thoughts away, but even though Pyra had earned the forgiveness of his king and apparently the others in the community, Ivy was not as quick to extend her good graces toward him. The journey that she had gone on since arriving on Uoria just weeks before was far more difficult and trying than anything that she could have ever imagined, and much of that was the fault of Pyra and the warriors who followed him with such devotion.

When Ivy first planned on coming to the planet to be with the scientist whose research assistant she had been for a couple of years, she had envisioned an exciting and thrilling opportunity that would allow her to use her knowl-edge and skill in a useful way while also having the unique chance to explore a new planet and encounter a species that she had only ever heard of, but never seen. Being a part of a university exchange program didn't seem like anything that could possibly be threatening. In fact, it seemed like the safest option for venturing off of Earth and seeing and experiencing new things while also pursuing the career path that she was so passionate about.

Almost as soon as she arrived, however, she found that her thoughts of this experience were nothing like what she was actually going to experience. Within moments of the university shuttle landing, all of her expectations of her time on the planet and her plans for what she and George would accomplish together shattered. Creia and Theia, the king and queen of the Denynso compound, had not been the welcoming people Ivy had heard that they could be. Instead, they showed cold anger and distrust toward her because she had arrived without giving them the notification that they expected from all who arrived on the planet. She had accepted this reaction with as much grace as she could, understanding that in her rather spontaneous decision to join George on Uoria even after telling him that she wouldn't be able to because of the timing, she had gone against the strictly held rules of the Denynso and offended their sense of tradition and regulation. When George stepped forward and acted as her representative, asking forgiveness of the rulers and appealing to them to allow her to stay on the planet rather than facing punishment and exile as they could have done, she felt a sense of relief. Had she known what she was going to face after that moment, that relief might not have been so pronounced.

She had come to Uoria with visions of the massive warriors and thoughts of learning about them and the amazing physical abilities of their kind, as well as the plant life of the planet and what role the environment played in the truly astonishing strength and power of the Denynso. Instead, she arrived in a compound that had been largely emptied and that felt oppressed under a low-hanging sense of worry and urgency that made the entire atmosphere of the surroundings feel anxious. Very soon she learned that the warriors had left the compound in a quest to explore the rest of the planet and find out what other species lived there in an effort to protect themselves and the impending future generation from whatever threats might be there. Though the goals of the university exchange program were still there, she found that the efforts had largely halted because of the war with the Klimnu that had burned through the compound and the new urgency to learn more about Uoria.

Then rather than concentrating on creating lesson plans for those Denynso interested in learning more about Earth and the people who were there, and gathering information to bring back to Earth to share with the rest of the university and possibly publish into their first co-authored studies, Ivy and George found themselves working with the human women. The warriors had contacted them after finding a settlement in which all of the people were frozen in place, seeking help finding a solution. While it was exciting in a way to be working on such a dynamic and unusual problem, Ivy felt like she had been thrown into something that she hadn't anticipated all because Pyra had decided that the warriors should head out into the planet to find out more about it.

Though she didn't realize it then, that had been when the smallest seeds of animosity for Pyra had been planted. She had heard that he was a powerful and impressive warrior, a leader that no one could deny and who could bring down any army. She had been so excited to meet him and compare what she had heard of him to reality, but she almost immediately found herself disappointed. When they went to the settlement, there was no time to get to know the warriors and learn about the Denynso. Instead, they were thrown into conflict, saving the people who were dying in front of them and struggling to come to terms with the discovery that these people, the humans who were on the planet even though the common knowledge was that there had been no humans on Uoria until they started to arrive in the compound at the invitation of the Denynso decades after this settlement was established, were actually the survivors of a long-lost mission from Earth that had been sabotaged by a species that Ivy hadn't even heard of until then.

The true feelings of disgust and fury toward the Denynso leader, however, had built after she had met Maxim and they discovered through a horrible reaction of his skin that the Mikana, a group of ethereally beautiful men who had come from a kingdom that once had friendly relations with the settlement, were in fact the creatures that had turned into the Klimnu. Finding out that the beings that they thought that they had eradicated in their final painful battle in fact still existed, if even in their whole and beautiful form, enraged Pyra, and Ivy watched him dissolve from the strong, rational leader he was supposed to be to one so overcome with hatred and fear that he took all of the Mikana, including Maxim, hostage and threatened to kill them all to prevent them from ever having the opportunity to become the gruesome enemies that had caused them so much hurt and left them in even greater terror. However, the Denynso would never admit that it was fear that was influencing them.

Everyone seemed to have overcome this turmoil as soon as they had brought Maxim and the Mikana leader Rey to Creia and the focus turned from Pyra's violence and aggression to his admitting his wrongdoing in the wake of the shock of Creia admitting he hadn't told everyone the full truth of the origins of the Denynso, and Rey stepping forward to help Eden give birth to her son. Ivy had not been so quick to forgive. She wanted to. She wanted to be able to put it all behind her and move forward with the others, but when she looked at Pyra she still saw the man who tried to kill the man she loved, and who had been so quick to sacrifice an entire species just for the transgressions of some of their ancestors. It just wasn't in her to let go of the horror and the anger that it caused, even when Pyra sank to his knees in front of his father and king to ask for forgiveness, and even when she saw the tears in his eyes and knew that he truly was feeling regret at the way that he had behaved. She knew that he felt remorse, but it wasn't enough for her. She still didn't feel like she could trust him completely.

2

Ivy felt Maxim's hand cover hers and their fingers intertwine. She took her eyes away from Pyra and brought them to Maxim's beautiful face, but noticed that his eyes seemed etched with something slightly dark and troubled. Concern constricted her belly and she immediately felt herself become defensive again. She tightened her grip on his hand and turned her body slightly so that it faced him more than the table in front of her.

"Maxim?" she said, searching his eyes for some explanation of the expression. "What is it? Is everything alright?"

"I need to talk to you about something," he said and the sound of his voice reflected the strain on his face.

"What's wrong?"

"Rey and some of the others are leaving in the morning to go back to the settlement to free the rest of the Mikana and tell them about our new alliance with the Denynso."

"I know," Ivy said. "I'm sorry that the shuttle to go to Earth is going to be arriving too soon for you to be able to go to the settlement."

Maxim nodded slightly.

"That's just the thing," he said. "I want to go to the settlement."

Ivy shook her head at him, her eyes narrowing slightly.

"What do you mean you want to go? The university is sending their fastest shuttle. There's no way that you would be able to get to the settlement and back here in time in order to catch it."

"I know. It's just that I really feel like I should be there. I feel that it is my responsibility to be with my people and see this through. I was in there with them, remember."

"Yes, I know," Ivy said, her grip on his hand faltering somewhat, "and I'm the one that came and got you out of it so that we could run away."

"But we didn't get away, Ivy. We came back and because we came back we were able to help these two species come together. I want to be there when the rest of the group is freed from the meeting hall. I want to be a part of the rebuilding."

"What about all of the plans that we had?" Ivy asked. "What about Samira and Ty's wedding?"

"You aren't even in the wedding," Maxim said. "You barely know them."

"That's not the point," Ivy said.

She knew that her voice was rising and Maxim looked around at the other tables to see if anyone was listening in.

"Can we go outside?" he asked.

Ivy dropped his hand to the table and stood, stepping backwards over the bench so that she could walk out of the banquet hall and down the front steps of the main building into the clearing at the center of the Denynso compound. It felt strange to step out into the night and look around to see no one around them. From the time that she arrived on the compound it had been made clear to her that she was not to move about the compound without the guard and protector who Creia had assigned to her, and though she had spent time on her own and with Maxim once they arrived at the settlement, she had not been without Zsilvia in the time that she had spent at the compound.

"You told me that you understood why I want to get back to Earth. You said that you wanted to go with me."

"I do want to go with you, Ivy."

Ivy took off at a fast, long stride across the clearing, heading toward the small row of houses where she had settled after first arriving.

"Apparently you don't."

"Are you allowed to go back to your house without telling anyone?" Maxim asked, the sound of his voice only slightly teasing. "Don't you still have to tell Zsilvia or at least George that you're going somewhere?"

"I am tired of telling anyone where I'm going or not being able to go where I want to go and do what I want to do," she said, whirling around to face him. "That's exactly why I am so ready to get off of this planet and back home. I don't have to have a guard and protector there. I move about how I please and no one tells me what to do."

"I'm sure that they will not force you to keep with a guard and protector for much longer. The others do not have them."

"The others are mated to their guards. They don't need them anymore because they are locked into them for life. I don't belong here, Maxim."

"What do you mean?"

"I am not part of them. I am not Denynso, and I am not the mate of one of the warriors or other men like the other human women are. Even George came here and bonded to Zsilvia. I'm an outsider."

"Because you fell in love with me?" Maxim asked, turning away and taking a few steps away from where Ivy stood.

"No." Ivy regretted saying the words as soon as she heard them come out of her mouth and saw the hurt on Maxim's face. "I am just not one of them. Uoria, from what I've seen of it, is beautiful and there are wonderful things to learn, but I wasn't ready for all of this. There has just been too much war and confusion for me."

"That's exactly why I have to get back to the settlement and then back to the kingdom," Maxim told her.

"What do you mean?"

"I'm tired of being confused. I'm tired of not knowing what is happening, even in my own family. I need to get to my brother and talk to him about our father. He might remember things that I don't that might be able to help me figure out the Order and what they have to do with the Klimnu."

"You don't even know who's in it or who controls it. Why does it matter what they knew?"

"My father died because of the Order and it had something to do with the Klimnu. My mother has never been the same since then. I need to know what happened to him and what the Order has been doing." Maxim suddenly turned to Ivy and took both of her hands in his, pulling her closer to him and staring into her eyes. "My mother told me, told us, that if we were going to have a life we had to stand up for ourselves and we had to finish what we started. I have to go back, Ivy. I have to finish this. I want to be with you. Please believe me. I love you like I never knew that love existed and I do not want to spend a moment of my life without that love, but I have to do this. I won't be able to move forward with our life until I get the answers to my questions and I am truly able to put all of this behind me."

Ivy felt herself melting at his words. As much as she wanted to go home, she knew that Maxim was absolutely right. With everything that they had found out about the Order and their involvement with the Klimnu only came more questions. Creia's revelations about another Denynso compound that had existed right on the other side of the rock ledges along the edge of the current compound had only brought up more confusion and more gaps in their information. She knew that she couldn't ask him to put all of that aside just so that he could go to Earth with her. He needed to resolve those areas of his life so that he could put them behind him and move ahead with her.

"Alright," she said, returning the tightness of his grasp on her hands. "We don't have to wait here for the shuttle and go back to Earth with the others. We'll join Rey and go back to the settlement."

"We?" Maxim asked, some of the familiar sparkle returning to his eyes.

Ivy nodded.

"You don't think that I would let you go through this without me, do you?" she asked. Ivy leaned forward and touched her lips to his softly. "If it wasn't for how much I love you, you never would have come into contact with those flowers and no one would have found out about the Mikana and the Klimnu. I suppose that makes us largely responsible for this mess."

Maxim laughed and returned her kiss. In that kiss she could still taste the new and exciting warmth of him that she had indulged in with such pleasure and intensity when they made love in the flowers outside of the Nyx 23 settlement. It was the reaction of his skin with those flowers, just as it had been with the rogue Mikana who had split off from the rest of the kingdom so many years before, that had shown the evolution from the Mikana to the Klimnu and that had started the storm of backlash from the Denynso warriors.

"I suppose we are," he said, and then the darkness returned, "but they would have found out. Eventually the Order would have made it known, I just don't know how."

"It doesn't matter if you know how now," Ivy said. "We will figure it out together. Come on," she said with a sigh of resignation, "we should probably go tell Creia about our plans. I wouldn't want to cause another problem doing something impulsive."

Ivy saw a mischievous flicker in Maxim's eyes and felt him drop one of her hands so that he held her fingertips. He started backing toward the houses, guiding her with a gentle pull on her fingers.

"Do you think that they are going to notice that you're gone?" he asked.

"I don't think so."

"Not even Zsilvia?"

"She and George are pretty wrapped up in each other right now."

"Good."

Maxim gave a hint of a smile, bit into his bottom lip, and turned so that he walked forward toward the houses, still pulling her gently along behind him. They walked in silence until they got to her house and he led her inside.

"What are you doing?" Ivy asked as they stepped inside and Maxim turned to press her back against the door.

He leaned forward and pressed his body to hers, covering her with himself so that she felt the pressure of his entire body touching hers and the insistence of a hardening erection nudging into her belly. His mouth crushed down on hers, drawing her tongue in against his. He kissed her until she was breathless and then pulled his mouth far enough way that he could speak but so she could still feel his lips brush against hers as he spoke.

"I'm being spontaneous. If you are going to get into trouble for spontaneity, it might as well be worth it."

Ivy smiled into the kiss that returned to her mouth and wrapped her arms around Maxim's neck as his hands came to her hips and pulled her up against him so that the pressure of his erection was even stronger in her belly. The feeling made her mouth water and she felt her body responding to him, aching for him. They hadn't had the opportunity to be alone nearly enough in the last few days for her and now that nearly everyone else in the compound was at the meeting hall, she felt like she could barely control herself. She needed him like she could never have imagined needing anyone.

Her hands dug into Maxim's back and she felt him press her back so that their bodies parted. He was shaking his head and Ivy looked at him quizzically.

"What?" she asked.

"Slow," he whispered and eased her arms away from his neck.

"Why?" she asked.

"Slow," he repeated.

Maxim's mouth touched the side of her neck and made its way down to the curve of her shoulder. As he kissed along her skin, his fingers moved to the row of buttons along the front of her shirt. He moved with torturously slow precision, opening the buttons gradually from the hem up so that he revealed the trembling skin of her belly first, then her ribs, and finally her breasts. His breath brushed along the swells of her breasts above the low-cut lace cups of her bra and she felt her skin tingle at the sensation. Maxim brought his mouth further down and followed the trail of his breath with her lips. Occasionally his tongue slipped out to glaze along her skin. The touch was bringing her desire for him to a fevered pitch, but he continued his patient, exacting exploration of her as he carefully pulled her just far enough away from the door to ease her shirt off of her shoulders and down her arms.

Ivy wrapped her fingers around the bottom of his shirt and pulled it up, forgoing the ties at the front and tossing it aside as quickly as she could so that she could access the warm, smooth skin beneath. He stood still long enough to allow her to lean forward and touch a series of kisses along the center of his chest. She could feel his heartbeat beneath her lips and could smell his intoxicating scent on his skin. After a moment Maxim took her by her upper arms and led her back against the door again. His hands smoothed around her ribcage until they reached the hooks of her bra and could unlatch it. He drew in a breath as he peeled the lace away from her body, revealing her desire-swollen breasts and darkened, taut nipples.

Maxim lowered himself to his knees and Ivy buried her fingers in his hair as he covered one breast with his mouth. One hand came up to cradle the swell as his tongue flicked over her nipple, encircling it and sucking tenderly as his other hand ran down the center of her belly to release the button on the front of her pants and ease down the zipper. Ivy stepped out of her shoes and lifted her hips away from the door so that Maxim could undress her further. She had forgone wearing anything under the pants when she got dressed that morning and Maxim made a sound of appreciation when she was finally bare in front of him.

She groaned when she felt his mouth move to the other

breast and repeat the same attention that he had given the first, and then start his slow progression down the center of her belly. The tip of his tongue dipped into her navel and she whimpered as a new wave of intense desire shot through her body and settled between her legs. She could feel herself getting wet and warm, preparing for him as he continued his kisses down her body.

Finally his mouth reached the apex of her thighs and Ivy felt Maxim's tongue delve through her folds in a long, slow lick that nearly brought her to her knees. The strands of his hair felt soft and thick in her fingers as she tightened her grip and held his head steady, desperate for more of the dizzying feeling. His hands moved to her hips so that he could hold her as he continued to coax her with the tip of his tongue. After a few moments he moved one hand down so that it tucked behind Ivy's knee and urged it away, parting her thighs and giving himself easier access to her. Maxim's tongue slid deeper and Ivy cried out at the intense feeling, her hips lifting off of the door to meet his mouth. He responded by cupping her butt in his hands so that he could tilt her pelvis forward toward him, allowing him even greater ability to explore her core.

Suddenly Maxim's tongue delved inside her, eliciting a scream. Rather than relenting, Maxim continued, swirling his tongue within her as he brought one of his hands forward so that he could massage the hypersensitive pearl of flesh at her peak. Ivy's head fell back against the door and she closed her eyes, surrendering herself to the incredible feelings Maxim was creating within her. His tongue eased out of her body and moved up so that the tip mimicked how his thumb had touched. She heard the sound of him easing out of his pants and the sound only worked to make her need for him greater.

His masterful worship of her body was bringing her close to the edge at incredible speed and Ivy could hear her own sounds pouring out of her as her hips rolled involuntarily against his mouth. She could feel how attuned he was to her body, adjusting and changing his touch in the slightest ways but so that she felt herself rapidly losing control. Just at the moment when she could feel herself spiraling into oblivion, Maxim bounded to his feet, swept one of her legs up to his hip, and sank inside of her. As soon as his body entered hers, Ivy felt her walls contract around him and she let out a strangled cry as her orgasm washed over her, pulling him deeply within her as he rolled his hips in long strokes to meet each of the waves that pulsed through her.

She was starting to come down from her climax when Maxim lifted her higher and tucked her against him so that she could wrap her legs around his hips. He turned and carried her into the living room, carefully laying her down on the sofa. She gazed up at him, savoring the feeling of him so hard and deep inside of her. Ivy released her legs, allowing one to drape over the back of the sofa and the other to hang over the side so that her toes touched the floor. The position opened her to Maxim fully and she could see the intensity of his desire for her flare in his eyes.

Maxim moved his body up so that he hovered over her, allowing Ivy to gaze into his eyes as he drove deeper into her. The muscles on his arms on either side of her bulged and strained against his skin as he rocked against her, groaning with each intense thrust. Ivy brought her hands to his back, allowing them to glide over skin slick with sweat as she savored the feeling of his muscles tightening and shifting beneath. As Maxim's thrusts became more insistent, his pace quickening and intensifying along with the sounds that came from deep in his throat, Ivy could feel herself moving closer and closer to another climax. She lifted her hips toward him, adjusting the angle just enough that he touched her back wall with every stroke and created a sensation that hummed through her body. Suddenly he gave one hard push and held himself as deep within her as he could get, tossing his head back and roaring as Ivy felt his hard cock throb.

The sensation of him filling her sent her toppling over the edge into her own orgasm and she felt her body squeeze down on him, milking him until they both collapsed into each other's arms, their ragged breath rising around them and their bodies seeming to meld together into one existence. Ivy had never experienced this level of closeness to anyone; the sense that their very souls were connected as much as their bodies were, and that Maxim was now completely, inextricably a part of her.

Ivy felt Maxim kissing along the curve of her neck as he rested his head on her, his body pressing down onto hers so that she felt fully enveloped in him. She wrapped her arms around him and sighed, touching a kiss to his shoulder before letting her eyes drift close and the feeling of him take her away. The rest of the compound was just going to have to miss them for a little while.

3

____

"Are you alright?" Lynx asked, coming to sit beside Rain at the table where she was completely alone.

Rain looked up at him as if coming out of a deep thought and then at the empty places around the table like it startled her to realize that no one else was sitting at the table. He wondered how long she had been sitting there by herself and felt a hint of worry. His mate had seemed to be struggling slightly since they left the settlement, and he felt like she was holding something back from him that she didn't want to talk about, as if she was still processing through it so carefully in her own mind that she didn't feel like she could put the proper words to it, even to him. He touched her back with one hand and felt her relax into the touch. Even though it had been a few weeks since they were able to wake her from the locked state that the Covra had put her and the rest of the Nyx 23 settlement into using a recording of Samira's voice, he still felt privileged and relieved each time he saw her move or heard her voice.

It had seemed like an eternity for him while he was

waiting for her to wake up. From the moment that he first discovered her, lying in the bed where she had gone to sleep for a nap one evening and was attacked by the Covra, he had known that this beautiful woman was intended to be his mate. Though he didn't understand it, he simply knew that Rain was meant to be his, and that no matter what it took he had to either figure out a way to free her from the locked state, or live throughout the rest of his life alone and longing for her, knowing that he was never going to feel the love and connection of a mate with anyone else. The wait had been excruciating as he visited her day after day, sleeping beside her in bed though she never moved, and talking to her constantly though she never spoke, and he didn't even know if she ever would. What had been even more excruciating than wondering if they would ever find a way to overcome the locking of the Covra and bring her back into conscious existence, was wondering if she would ever be able to understand his feelings for her and return them.

He understood that she was from a different time, that she may be frightened and confused when she woke up and not be able to comprehend what had happened to her, or life in a time one hundred years after she tucked herself beneath her flowered blanket and closed her eyes, but he had to try. He couldn't deny then what he was feeling for her and the sense of duty and responsibility to protect her even as they discovered that the people of the settlement were being used by the Covra as incubators for their next generation. Lynx had been there at that moment, he had been one of the first things that she had seen when finally freed from the bonds that the Covra had put her in and held her captive for decades before Lynx was even born. He would never forget how he felt in that moment, hanging in it like her breath had crystallized around him and was holding him still while she gazed at him, evaluating him, trying to understand what had happened and who he was.

Even more he would never forget what it was like when she told him that even though she couldn't open her eyes or respond to him, that she had been able to hear him talking to her, and that the sound of his words had been an incredible comfort to her. They had soon discovered that the reason she was able to hear him but not wake up fully was that the only thing that would break the locking was listening to one of her own kind speaking. The voices of the Denynso were close enough that it started to draw her out of the frozen state, but it could not bring her fully back into consciousness. It was not until she had heard Zuri's voice through the compact as Bannack communicated with Loralia and the others that she had begun to show any signs of life. It had been Zsilvia who had suggested that they use the recording of Samira's voice that she had given her mate Ty before the men left the compound. They played the recording continuously for hours, and soon the words drew her out of her lock, she breathed, and the blood started to flow through her veins once again.

Lynx knew in his mind that the toxins that the Covra used to lock the people of the settlement into place were gone and that she would never fall back into that frozen state again, but the fear always lingered in his heart that one day he would wake up and she would be gone again, lost into the years that had been swallowed by the Covra and beyond his reach. He was reminded of it each time he saw her sleep, and reminded of the cruel use that the Covra had of the people each time she removed her clothing. The scar from where Ciyrs had had to cut into her body to remove the eggs stood out gruesomely against the paleness of her stomach, a vicious reminder of the mere moments that had once separated her from a death more horrible than Lynx could have fathomed.

Despite the horror that that scar held, Lynx never shied away from it. He didn't allow it to have control over his thoughts or power over his adoration of her. When he saw it, he made a point to touch it. He ran his fingers along it as he made love to her and kissed it softly when she lay sleeping beside him. He hoped that in some way the tenderness of his skin against it would heal it more quickly and take away the darkness that the slightly raised ridge still seemed to hold.

Now as she returned staring at the table, seemingly engrossed in the pattern of the woodgrain, the intense fear and dread that had defined him in the days before she awoke threatened to settle over him again.

"What is it?" Lynx asked, touching her back again.

Rain returned her gaze to him and sighed.

"I don't know if I can do this, Lynx," she said softly.

Feeling alarmed both at her tone and her choice of words, Lynx slid slightly closer to her on the wooden bench and rested his arm around her waist. He was relieved when she leaned into him and briefly touched her forehead to his.

"What don't you think that you can do?" he asked.

"Go back to Earth."

Relief flooded over him, but was then replaced by confusion.

"I thought you wanted to go back to see it again."

"I know," Rain said, running her hands back through her hair. "And I thought that I did. When I first heard that a shuttle would be coming to bring some of the Denynso and the women to Earth, I was so excited. I thought that it was the perfect chance for me to finally get home and finish the mission that I started so long ago. I had this vision of me returning triumphant and getting to tell the story of what happened so that the world could finally know and I could get back to the life that I left behind."

Lynx felt his heart constrict painfully at those words. He knew what she was saying, but it sounded so painfully like she wanted to just forget everything that had happened since she arrived on the planet that he was terrified she was saying that she didn't care if that meant him as well.

"Of course," he managed, replying just so that she would know that he was listening to her.

"But then I really started thinking about it." Rain turned to him so that she straddled the bench facing him and opened her hands toward him as if showing him something that wasn't really there. "I started thinking about everything that the people of Earth now think of us and what it would do when they do find out what happened. It will change everything, Lynx. Everything. It will change the course of Earth's understanding of history, it will create animosity for a species that the people of Earth don't even know exist as far as I know, and it will make it so that more scientists and explorers and treasure hunters will want to come here. It will ravage Uoria and whatever is left of Penthos. I don't think that I can be a part of that."

"Maybe it won't be like that," Lynx offered, trying to comfort her. "I'm sure that it will be a surprise to them and that they will want to know more about what happened, but maybe it won't be so awful. You'll just have to be careful with how you tell it and make sure that you do everything that you can to protect the team as well as the planet."

"That's the thing, though, Lynx. It's not just my story to tell. There were dozens of people on that team. Now there are marriages and children, families that only exist because of what happened to us. There are people who really did die when the ship crashed, and even more who died in the conflict with the Covra and then in the hatching. Those lives matter. Even if they weren't lost in the way that the people on Earth think that they were lost, those people are still gone and their lives, their memories, matter. What we were able to build in the settlement matters. That was our world, Lynx. For fifteen years after we crashed, that was the comfortable, peaceful home that we created for ourselves, and now we're just thinking about abandoning it like it never existed. We're just going to leave behind our homes, our belongings. We're going to leave the bodies of the ones who died just buried alone out in the middle of the planet where no one goes."

"Not everyone is leaving, Rain. There were plenty of people in the settlement who didn't even want to come here much less go back to Earth. They want to stay."

"I think I do, too."

"Are you sure?"

"Yes. Earth was my home, but I have been here far longer than I was there, even if I don't remember most of it, and my loyalty has to lie with what we built here. I can't just abandon it. I can't pretend that those years didn't happen, and I can't pretend that showing back up on Earth is going to make it go away or that it is going to put things back to the way that they were before we left. That life that I left behind..." she sighed, looking down at the bench for a moment before lifting her eyes back to his, "that life is over. It will never be the same. It's behind me now and I will never be able to live that life again." She paused and reached up to cup Lynx's face with one delicate hand. "I wouldn't want to even if I could."

Lynx covered her hand with his, turning to press a kiss into her palm.

"Are you sure?"

"Yes. I love you, Lynx. I've loved you since before I had even seen you, and I will love you always. There is nothing that is waiting for me on Earth that could even begin to compare with what I have right here with you. I would love to have you live with me in the settlement, but even if we split our time between there and here at the compound, I will be happy as long as we're together."

"All I want is to be with you," Lynx said, leaning forward to rest her forehead against hers.

"It's also important to me to be there when they free the rest of the Mikana. It wasn't quite the same, but we were held captive by the Covra and our conflict with them for so long. We were sabotaged and threatened by the Valdicians and tormented by the Covra. We know what it's like to be taken over and to have no power, and I want to do for them what you and the rest of the Denynso did for us."

Lynx felt guilt wash over him.

"Even though it was the Denynso who are holding them captive?" he asked carefully.

Rain looked at him softly, the expression in her eyes telling him that she didn't hold any anger or judgment for him or for the rest of his kind despite everything that Pyra and some of the others had done.

"I will say the same thing now that Zuri said in the settlement about the Mikana and the Klimnu. Everyone has the potential for darkness." Lynx tried to look away but Rain turned his face back to hers insistently. "Everyone, Lynx. It wasn't the right way to go about it, but Pyra was doing what he thought was right for his kind. The way he went about it was completely wrong, but that's what makes situations like this so difficult. Sometimes it is hard to tell where what is right to one person ends and what is wrong to another person begins, or if, in truth, they are the same thing. What the Covra did was right and the way of perpetuating and protecting their kind in their eyes. That doesn't make it right and that doesn't mean that the suffering that they caused us wasn't real or should be forgotten, but it does give me more empathy than others might have."

"I don't understand."

"I went to Penthos with the rest of the Nyx 23 team because I knew in my heart that there was something going on on that planet that I believed was wrong and I felt like it was my responsibility to find out about it and end it. Ever since I found out that the military units went to the planet after they thought we disappeared and eradicated the Valdicians, though, I've been thinking about why they were doing what they were doing. We never found that out. We never even knew who the prisoners were, just that they were being held in an illegal prison camp. What we were fighting so hard against because we felt it was wrong, was something that was completely right to them, and what we did was wrong."

"So you don't think that the Valdicians should have been punished or that the Covra should have been killed?"

"No," Rain said, shaking her head, "that's not what I'm saying. All we have in this world is what we think is right, what we believe, and all we can do is live our lives the way that we think is right, knowing that along the way we are going to encounter others who see everything from their own perspective and think that what we are absolutely convinced is the right thing is actually the worst that could happen, and trying to see both sides."

"How could you be so generous?" Lynx asked.

It truly astonished him that this woman who had witnessed the brutality of a species holding another prisoner in horrific conditions, had her ship sabotaged and sent to a planet that she didn't know even existed, lost people she cared about in the crash, and had to rebuild her life thinking that she would never return to the country she knew and the people she loved, only to be taken over by a vicious species who inflicted pain by compelling the men to fight against one another and then left them for dead as the incubators and first meals of their children, could be so understanding. He would have thought that she would have been filled with hatred and wanted to seek revenge against every species that had hurt her, but she was looking at him with sincerity in her eyes that showed that even after every-thing she had gone through, even after she herself had been forced to fight and kill, she was willing to admit that there might be more to even the worst of creatures.

"I'm not being generous, Lynx. I don't like what happened to me. I don't feel love and kindness toward the Valdicians or the Covra, but I don't think that Pyra and the Denynso are comparable to them. The Mikana might argue with me about that, but that is what I want to help avoid. I don't want there to be another war. I want what we were trying to accomplish before we saw the reaction on Maxim's skin and everyone realized that the Mikana became the Klimnu. I want this planet, the planet that I have devoted the majority of my life to and the planet that I now consider my home, to finally come together."

"That's a beautiful thought."

"I don't mean it to be beautiful."

Lynx was taken aback by the sudden harshness in Rain's voice.

"What?"

"I don't mean it to be beautiful. Yes, it would be wonderful it all of the species who live on Uoria could come together and cooperate, that the species could love each other freely and not have to worry about what anyone thinks." At that, Rain took Lynx's hands in hers and he intertwined their fingers, holding her hands tightly as he thought of the negativity that the couples had faced as the different species came together. "But the truth is the conflicts aren't over. The Denynso thought that the Klimnu were gone, completely eliminated from the planet, didn't they?"

"Yes, but we didn't know about the Mikana. We didn't know anything about what they were before they were Klimnu except for what Leia was able to tell us from her time in the prison."

"That's my point, though, Lynx. You didn't know. You believed that the threat was gone, so when you found out that it might still be there, even if it was in a form that wasn't truly threatening at all, it created absolute panic. What if that's the same for the Covra or the Valdicians? I don't think that Uoria is safe."

"Then why do you want to stay?"

"Because I believe if we all came together and stopped letting misunderstandings and fear get in our way, that Uoria could be safe. We could protect it and ensure that it stays protected. There is more to this galaxy than Earth and Uoria, and we have to be ready for that. Besides, would you want to live on Earth?"

Lynx thought about the question for a moment. He had never considered living anywhere but on the Denynso compound. It had never even crossed his mind as a possibility.

"No."

"Exactly. This is your home. This is our home. I may want to visit Earth again someday just to see it and see how it's changed since we left, but for now I just want to go back to the settlement and finish this so we can move on."

"Alright," Lynx said, leaning forward to kiss her forehead. "If that's what you want, we'll go talk to Creia and tell him that we are joining the group going back to the settlement rather than going with the others."

"And you're ok with this?" she asked. "You don't want to go to Earth?"

"Like you said, we'll go there someday to visit. We don't need to go now. We're needed here."

4

Creia sat on the platform overlooking the banquet hall, his eyes moving from face to face as he watched the warriors, their mates, the humans, and the Mikana interacting. His children were among those faces, the most powerful and impressive of the warriors and those who had been destined from birth to lead just as he had. Up until now he had never thought about which of them would take his position when he was no longer king, or even if it would be one of his children. Though the original Denynso had passed the monarchy through birth, that had changed when the group divided and the current clan established themselves in this compound.

Rather than knowing who would ascend to the position of king after the end of the reign of the current king simply by birthright, it became a matter of earning that role. The man who would take over had to prove himself and demonstrate without realizing what he was doing that he was the only one within the clan who could rightfully rule. It was a tremendous feat and one that Creia simply assumed would occur without issue. Now in the wake of everything that had happened after the warriors and other men had left the compound for the first time to explore the planet, he wasn't as sure. He found himself worrying about when the time would come for the new king to step into his role and how that future king would prove himself. For the first time since he took over when he was even younger than his sons, he wondered if he had truly proven himself and if he had really been ruling the clan in the way that was truly best for them.

"Sir?"

Creia heard a voice speaking up at him from the foot of the platform. He recognized it as that of Maxim, the young Mikana man who had been the start of Pyra's rage about the Klimnu when he came into contact with the flowers that caused the same reaction that had begun on the Klimnu so many years before. He looked down and saw Maxim standing beside Ivy, his hand lightly holding hers between them as they gazed up at him. Looking down at him like that Creia could clearly remember the faces of the men who had come to him for help when they were going through their own horrific transformations. He could still see how their beauty was being ravaged by the quickly spreading reaction that left skin that was once smooth and soft pale, slimy, and sickly looking. He heard their voices reverberating through his mind, asking him to cure them.

He remembered the thoughts that had burned through his mind as he looked at them. They had already caused pain and heartache, and he had heard the plans they were making to take over the planet. He knew that the plan included his own compound. He didn't think that his clan would be safe if he healed them and allowed them to continue going about their lives after returning from the desolate planet that they had already all but destroyed. In those moments, he made the only decision that he thought he could. He told them that he would only heal them if they left Uoria and promised never to return.

He knew now that in that decision he had put himself, his children, and all of the Denynso, in incredible danger. Looking at Maxim, however, he knew that he had done what was right. Healing their skin wouldn't have changed what the Klimnu were. He could see the difference in Maxim's eyes. There was life and energy there that wasn't in the cold black eyes of the Klimnu. It was a difference that could seem so subtle but that meant everything.

"Yes, Maxim?" Creia said, stepping closer to the edge of the platform so that he could lean down to talk to the young man.

"Ivy and I have decided that we don't want to go to Earth on the shuttle when it comes."

"Oh?"

"We want to go back to the settlement so that I can be there to release my brother and the rest of our kind."

"Sir?"

Before Creia was able to answer Maxim, he heard Lynx. The warrior approached with the woman who he had released from the lock of the Covra and who he had taken as his mate.

"Yes, Lynx?"

"I'm sorry to interrupt, but I overheard Maxim saying that he wants to return to the settlement rather than joining the others going to Earth."

"Yes, that's what he was just telling me, and I –"

"We'd like to go, too."

Lynx cut him off and Creia closed his mouth slowly. He evaluated both of the men, searching their sincere, earnest faces and the way that they stood confidently in front of him.

"You want to join the group going back to the settlement to release the members of the Mikana kingdom?" Creia said, carefully repeating the sentiment that Maxim had expressed to ensure that Lynx really understood what he was volunteering himself for.

"Yes. I think that I could offer more being here than going to Earth right now."

Creia nodded. He looked from Lynx to Maxim, and then to Rain.

"And you?" he asked.

Rain nodded and Creia found himself caught by the strangeness of her lovely eyes, coppery hair, and smooth, unaged skin. It was somewhat unnerving to look at someone who he appeared so much younger than he was, only to remind himself that she had been alive, if not suspended for much of the time, for more than a century.

"I know that I come from Earth originally, but I have come to think of Uoria as my home and I don't want to leave it. I want to go back to the settlement and work on rebuilding it now that the threat of the Covra is over."

"And you, Ivy?" Creia asked.

Though his first impression of the young, willowy girl had not been positive, he had grown to admire her strength and fortitude. When faced with challenges and demands that would have sent many people running back to him and begging for the first shuttle off of the planet, she had confronted them fully and been an integral part of the resolutions. Even though he knew that she hadn't become a part of them like the other women had and was not comfortable on the compound, he felt a level of respect for her and wanted to ensure that she was making a decision that she felt comfortable with.

"Yes, sir," she responded. "It is important to Maxim that

he be there now and my place is with him. I'll stay here for as long as he needs to."

Creia gave a single nod, accepting the selfless gesture.

"I will allow all of you to join the group returning to the settlement. If you change your minds and want to go to Earth to join the others," he took a breath, "or to stay, I will make the arrangements for you."

"Thank you," Maxim and Lynx said together.

The two women smiled and nodded at him, reaching out to take their mates and guide them away from the platform. Creia had a strange feeling as he watched them walk away, Maxim and Ivy walked toward the table where the others who would be departing the next morning for the settlement sat, discussing their plans, and Rain and Lynx toward the main door to the building, likely heading back to Lynx's house to begin preparing themselves.

"You're worried about them, aren't you?" Theia asked, coming to his side and wrapping one hand around his arm.

Creia turned to his mate and accepted the kiss that she offered him. He nodded, turning his gaze back to the room.

"They're fighting my fight," he said.

"What fight is that, Creia?"

"They are trying to protect the planet."

"Is that your fight?"

"Hasn't it always been?"

"I don't know, Creia. I've never known."

Theia touched a kiss to the side of her mate's neck and walked away. Creia replayed her words in his mind. His mate had always been able to read exactly how he was feeling, but rarely would she tell him what she thought. Instead she would turn the situation around so that he was forced to truly think about it himself and interpret what he was thinking and feeling. While this often helped him to go deeper into what was happening and figure things out from a perspective that he might not have had otherwise, at that moment it only worked to make him more uncomfortable. He didn't want to delve any further into what he was feeling or the memories that these feelings were dredging up. The last few days since the group arrived back from the settlement had been difficult enough and forced him to confront issues that he thought would remain buried forever. He didn't know if he was ready to have to deal with even more.

5

"I promise you, you're going to be fine."

Samira reached out and patted Johnathan's hand, trying to offer the aging man comfort. He looked at her with pale grey eyes and gave a slightly weak smile. She was sitting at one of the long tables in the banquet hall with several of the people who were planning on heading to Earth on the shuttle that was scheduled to arrive in just a few days. Most of her thoughts were on her wedding and the excitement of finally having that experience with Ty, but she was also feeling concern for the members of the Nyx 23 group who had decided that it was time that they return to Earth. Only a few of the Nyx 23 group had come to the decision that they would return to Earth and try to start their lives again. Even though there was a sense of great excitement about their long-awaited trip back home, there was also a sense of worry and nervousness.

"How different is it going to be?" Johnathan asked.

Samira tried to come up with an answer. The idea of being gone from the planet for more than one hundred years and then returning was something that she couldn't even begin to fathom. The truth was that she had been on Uoria for only a matter of months and she was already concerned that Earth would be different when she returned, or that she wouldn't remember how to go about her life not living on the compound with the Denynso. She couldn't imagine what these people were going through wondering if they would ever be able to fit back in on the planet that they had left behind anticipating only being gone for a few weeks and instead crashing on an unknown planet and having to recreate their lives there. The thought was frightening, but she didn't want to let that on. They were already unnerved enough and she didn't feel like she needed to make it even worse for them.

"I can't really answer that," Samira said truthfully. "I only know what your time there was like from books and movies. I can tell you that it is most certainly different, and that you will have to get used to it. With all of the attention that you are going to get just from coming back to the planet alive after all of this time, though, you will definitely not be alone. Everyone will be there to help you figure everything out."

"What if we don't want the attention?" Brandy, a woman sitting near the end of the table asked.

Samira looked at her and felt a pang of compassion for her and for the others. She could see the nervousness in Brandy's eyes, but could also hear the defensiveness in her voice. In their excitement to discover that the team that they had been taught throughout their entire schooling had disappeared during their most dangerous mission had actually survived, Samira and the other women had just assumed that the Nyx 23 team would be looking forward to getting back to Earth and telling their story. It hadn't occurred to her that they might be reluctant to share what had happened to them, and that they might not be ready for the world to know everything that they had gone through, or to handle all of the attention that would come with their return.

"Then you don't have to have it," Samira told her. "No one is going to force you to tell anyone what happened or even to tell anybody who you are. You can just go back to Earth and settle in, and then after a while when you think that you might be ready, then you can tell them. You are going back home for yourselves, not for anyone else, and you don't have to do or say or live up to anything."

She could see the relief in Brandy's eyes as the woman looked at her for a few beats and then turned to exchange glances with the other people from her team sitting around the table. They leaned in close to each other and she heard them starting to whisper about the situation, discussing amongst themselves how they wanted to handle telling people who they were and what they would say about what had happened to them.

Samira felt a touch on her back and looked up to see Ty standing beside her. She smiled at him and took the hand that he offered to her. The group at the table was exploring the idea of going back and not saying anything to anyone until they were able to really talk to the rest of the crew and create a united front when Samira stood, stepped over the wooden bench, and let Ty lead her out of the meeting hall.

The evening was deepening into night as they walked across the empty center of the compound and toward Ty's shop. She remembered the brief time that she had spent in the small visitor house chosen for her by Creia after Zuri had contacted him to let him know that she was going to come back to Uoria with her. Though she had originally thought that she would be in that visitor house for the duration of her time on the planet, she had in fact only spent a few days there before she realized how deeply in love with Ty she was and convinced the tremendous man to admit that he loved her just as much. Though he had been reluctant because of her age, once Ty relented to the feelings that he had for her, his passion and devotion were unlike anything Samira had ever known existed.

They stepped into Ty's shop and she took a deep breath of the lingering smell of fresh bread that hung in the air. Despite his massive size, incredible strength, and rare and special ability to move things with his mind that was completely unique to him among the Denynso, Ty was not truly a warrior. Just as the warriors were born to fulfill the duty of fighting to defend the compound and their kind, Ty was born with the purpose of being the nurturer of the clan. His role in the clan was to prepare food and take care of the warriors when they returned from battle injured. Ciyrs did the actual healing, but Ty was the one who would make sure that they had the care and support they needed to get better.

Ty guided her through the shop and into the attached house that they had shared since they completed their bond. They walked through the darkness and up the tall flight of steps that led from the main room of the house up to the long hallway that featured their bedroom and bathroom. Once they were in the bedroom, he turned her around and started undressing her. He still hadn't said a word to her, but she gave herself over to him completely, allowing him to quickly remove her shirt and then untie the knot at her hip that held her skirt in place as she stepped out of her shoes. She released her bra and dropped it to the side as Ty slid her panties off of her hips and down her legs.

As soon as they were off, Samira sank down to her knees

and went to work releasing the laces on Ty's pants while he removed his shirt. Wrapping her hand around his already surging erection, Samira took him into her mouth and luxuriated in the deep groan the stroke of her tongue drew from his throat. His hand tucked around the back of her head and she took him in further, letting her tongue stretch to the base and then swirl around the tip, gathering the salty-sweet fluid. Letting the pressure of his hand guide her, she used her hand to stroke the base of his cock while she concentrated the slow, worshipful sucking of her mouth on the tip.

Ty's hips were rolling subtly, pressing her deeper into his mouth and his sounds were growing more intense when he suddenly took her by her upper arms and pulled her to her feet. His mouth crushed down on hers and their tongues tangled as Ty led Samira back toward the bed with the pressure of his body. Just as Samira felt the backs of her thighs touch the edge of the mattress, Ty pulled his mouth away from hers and tipped her forward so that she landed on her stomach on the bed. She felt him climb over her, his body enveloping hers and his tongue running up her spine as he used one knee to nudge her thighs apart.

Ty's hand tucked beneath her hips and lifted them slightly. She groaned as she felt the tip of his erection stroke along her wet core, coaxing her to open up further for him. Samira pressed back with her hips, encouraging him to enter her, and felt him finally fill her. Her body stretched to welcome him and she gripped the blankets in front of her, moaning at the deep, fulfilling sensation of their bodies coming together. As soon as he settled completely into her, Samira felt Ty start to move his hips. His first few strokes were long and deep, nurturing her as he kissed along her shoulder. Then his pace quickened until he was pounding into her with such intensity she couldn't control the cries of pleasure pouring out of her.

A shattering orgasm shuddered through her and she arched into him, pressing him even deeper into her until she felt him surge forward and spill into her. Ty held himself in place for several long seconds then collapsed down onto Samira's back, gathering her into his arms and rolling onto his side so that he cradled her against his body. She could feel him still nestled within her and she wriggled her hips back against him to enjoy more of the feeling.

Ty kissed her temple and wrapped his arm around her so that their bodies entwined completely.

"I love you," he whispered.

Samira sighed contentedly and turned her head to kiss his arm.

"I love you, too."

"I can't wait to marry you." Samira's heart fluttered and she nodded. She felt Ty's arm tighten around her slightly. "Is something wrong?" he asked.

"Should we really be doing this?"

Ty sat up suddenly on his hip, causing Samira to tip back so that she was on her back staring up at him.

"What do you mean? Do you not want to marry me anymore?"

Samira reached up and cupped his cheeks with both hands.

"Of course I want to marry you," she said. "I've always wanted to marry you. I'm just worried that with everything that has been going on if planning a wedding is really what we should be doing."

"Why?"

"You don't think that it feels disrespectful or tasteless to come home after all the fighting and death, and then go back to Earth for a big party? Should we postpone it for a while to give everyone a chance to get over everything that we've just gone through?"

Ty pulled her up so that she was sitting facing him and rested his forehead against hers for a moment.

"I think that it is exactly what we should be doing," he said.

"Really?" Samira asked, pulling back so that she could look into his glowing orange eyes.

"Absolutely," he said. "After everything that we've gone through, what we need is something hopeful. We all need to be reminded of what it is to be just happy. This wedding isn't just for you and me. It's for all of us. This is something that no Denynso has ever experienced. For our kind, bonding with your mate is a very private thing. We watch our friends and family members go from being single, to experiencing the attraction of finding their mates, to being mated. It's a process that happens outside of the view of anyone else. We don't get to celebrate the joy of them coming together. Our wedding is going to let them celebrate with us, and it's going to be a fun and happy distraction from everything else. It will represent hope and unification. I think that it is exactly what everyone needs."

6

____

"It feels different down here now," Loralia said, gazing around the cavern.

Bannack dropped down from the vine he had climbed down so that he stood beside Loralia where she was pressed to the stone wall of the cavern. She reached for his hand, taking it in hers so that she could feel the connection between them as she tried to get used to the new feeling of the space that had always been her home. This system of caverns and chambers had been her home since birth and she had lived there completely alone for several years before the Klimnu came and then the Denynso waged war against them right in that cavern. That is when she met Bannack and made the impulsive, love-compelled decision to climb out of the caverns for the first time in her life and experience the world above her.

"Why?" Bannack asked.

Loralia shook her head. She couldn't quite explain what was going through her mind. She knew that there was something that was not the same and that would never be the same.

"I never knew why my kind came down here," she said. "I knew that we weren't always down here. My grandmother had told me that we weren't always here and that there was a time when we lived above ground, but were forced to come down here because of another species. I didn't know what that meant until now. I didn't know what had caused the plague that they ran from or that killed all of them, and even though I still don't really understand how the arrival of the Valdicians caused it, everything that Creia told us has changed what I think about them and their memory."

Losing everyone that she knew and loved had been horrific, but Loralia had forced her feelings and memories to stay behind her. She had pushed them into the back of her mind and continued forward in her life alone, resigning herself to be the only one that would ever know about her kind and that the knowledge of their history would die with her. Now she didn't feel the same way. She had survived for a reason. She had gotten through the plague that had burned through the cavern and destroyed her species, which meant it was her responsibility to make sure that they were never forgotten.

"You're still wondering why the plague didn't kill you."

"Of course, I am. It doesn't make any sense. I was right there with everyone else. I didn't go anywhere different or do anything different. So how did I escape it? I don't even remember being sick at all. Not even a little bit. Everyone else got sick and were dead within just a few days, but I always stayed just as healthy. It doesn't make sense."

"What about Ty?" Bannack suddenly asked.

Loralia glanced at him quizzically as she removed the compact from her neck and opened it so that she could create a solid floor across the reflected sky in front of them.

"What do you mean?" she asked.

She held the compact in her palm and tilted it so that the mirrors reflected the stones across the reflected sky and created a path where she could step.

"How do you feel when you are near him?"

"I can't honestly remember spending much time with him," she admitted. "I know that I have, but not really enough that I could tell you if it made me feel any different. Why do you ask?"

"Don't you remember what Creia said?"

Loralia stepped off of the final stone of the path onto the ground across the sky and turned sharply back to look at Bannack who was making his way carefully across the stones. She hadn't thought about it until that moment, but suddenly she remembered more of what Creia had said. He hadn't just talked about her kind and how they had abandoned their home on the compound that the Denynso now inhabited to create their own home beneath the ground. He had also talked about the original Denynso compound just on the other side of the rocks at the edge of the compound and the two strange children that had been born to two Denynso women once the clan split and half moved onto the land above them now.

"He's a descendent of the Valdicians," she murmured.

"Distantly, but yes. He is the first one of the line that has shown any of the abilities of the Valdicians. That means that the bloodline is strong in him."

"So I might have some kind of reaction to him?"

"I don't know. I don't know how that worked, but Creia said that the sickness started when the Valdicians came, ended when they went away, and then came again when the Valdicians returned."

"How, though?" Loralia asked, the desperation growing

inside her. "It doesn't make any sense. My kind came down here to escape from the plague. No one even knew that we were down here. How did the Valdicians cause the plague to come back if they never came down here?"

Bannack shook his head and reached out to take her into his arms. She tucked her head against his chest, holding herself as close to him as she could so that she could take comfort in the strength of his arms and the beating of his heart. In that moment it felt like those were the only things that would stay the same, the only things that she could rely on.

"Do you want to skip the wedding?" Bannack asked.

Loralia thought about it for a moment, and then shook her head.

"No. I can't avoid him forever. Nothing has happened yet, and I've been living in the same area as him for far longer than my kind was near the Valdicians before they got sick."

The embrace ended and Loralia started deeper into the caverns. She didn't know what she was looking for or even why she had come down there with him. Something about getting the new information from Creia had drawn her back into the home that she had always known. It was like she could feel them more strongly than she had in years. She could almost hear their voices coming at her through the rocks, reminding her of the days of her childhood growing up there and never imagining what the world outside of the caverns held. In the months after the final death of the plague Loralia realized that she had separated herself so much from her kind and the life that she once had. She no longer followed the traditions or carried on with the ways that her parents had taught her.

Now that someone else had acknowledged them, now

that she knew the torment that her ancestors had gone through and the courage that they had shown as they recreated their lives in the chambers that they manipulated to mimic the land above them that they loved so deeply, but that they knew they would likely never see again, she felt as though she were stepping back into that existence. She no longer wanted to separate herself from who she was and where she came from, and it suddenly felt extremely important that she carry with her the legacy of all those who came before her.

She turned to Bannack.

"Do you remember when we first bonded and you asked me how my kind made their pairs?"

He nodded.

"Yes."

"I told you about the tying ceremony and you told me that you wanted us to do that someday."

"I remember."

"Do you still want to do it?"

"Of course I do, if you want to."

"I do," she said. "I didn't know if I did before, but I know how important it is to me now. I already feel completely bonded to you and wanting to have this ceremony has nothing to do with not feeling like you and I are connected. I just realized that I am all that is left of my kind now, but that if we ever have children, those children will be part of my line as well. They will carry on my species, at least in part, and they deserve to know who they are and where they come from. I am dedicated to the Denynso and I want our children to be proud of their lineage, but I also want them to be proud of my side as well. I owe it to my family and to our future to carry on the culture and traditions of my kind so that they are never forgotten."

Bannack ducked his head to kiss her.

"Then we will. We will get married the way that your family would have and when our children our born, they will know everything that came together to create them."

7

———

Eden tucked Lysander into the crook of her arm and nestled him close to her to nurse. His tiny hand rested against her chest and she felt the warmth of him settle through her skin. She sighed, feeling content in a way that she had never imagined, and ran a finger along her newborn son's soft cheek.

"Is he alright?"

Eden looked up to see Pyra standing in the doorway of the nursery, looking at her nervously. She smiled at her mate and nodded.

"Of course he is. He's just eating. How is everyone at the meeting hall?"

"They're fine," Pyra said, pushing off of the doorframe and stepping into the room. "They all asked about you and the baby. I talked to people about him who I haven't spoken to in probably a year."

Eden laughed.

"Babies will do that. There's something about a brand new little one that suddenly makes everyone feel closer."

Lysander's mouth fell away from Eden's breast and she looked down to find him asleep, the last remnants of milk bubbling out of his satisfied-looking mouth. She covered herself and took the small cloth from over her shoulder to wipe away the milk. Pyra came to her side and reached down for him with his tremendous hands. Just as she had envisioned when Lysander was still tucked comfortably within her, Eden could place the baby into Pyra's hands and he was fully enveloped, rested as safely in those palms as he was when his mother held him in his arms.

She watched as Pyra leaned down to touch a kiss to Lysander's head and felt a surge of tenderness rise within her. When she was on Earth she had never thought of herself as the type of woman who wanted to be a mother. She wasn't like the other girls who played with dolls and spent hours meticulously brushing and styling their hair, dressing them in those tiny clothes, and pretending to feed and change them. And she had never been the type of teenager or young woman who envisioned getting married and having children of her own one day. She had always been so much more invested in her schooling and then in her career, thoughts of anything else just weren't something that she felt like she had the time to entertain. That all changed when she met Pyra.

Though their initial meeting and the first bit of time that they knew each other had not gone smoothly, when they finally came together, she knew that he was everything that she had been missing in her life, and that she wanted to create her life there on Uoria with him. When she discovered she was pregnant, she had been incredibly shocked, but even more surprising to her than the fact that she was carrying the warrior's child was how happy and excited she felt about it. She had an unexplainable sense of pride knowing that she had his baby within her and that she would be the one who would bear the first member of the new generation of the Denynso. It felt like an incredible honor, but more importantly it felt like she was creating a family with Pyra that she had never known that she wanted, but now knew that she never wanted to live without.

Seeing Pyra cradling their baby and whispering to him with gentleness and sweetness that belied his huge body and rough impression made the world feel calm, comfortable, and complete. She now knew that everything she had gone through in her life leading up to the moment when she stepped onto the shuttle to come to Uoria, everything with her family, everything with Ryan, had been absolutely worth it.

"Lynx isn't coming to the wedding," Pyra said, looking over at Eden.

She stood from her chair and crossed to the basket of baby clothes that had been sitting on the changing table Ero had built for them.

"He isn't?" she asked, picking up one of the tiny blankets that the midwives had made for her and folding it carefully.

"No," Pyra said, adjusting his grip on Lysander so that the newborn was draped on his chest, his father's tremendous hand nearly engulfing his body as Pyra held him in place, "He, Rain, Maxim, and Ivy have all decided that they aren't going to go back to Earth. They're going to leave with the group tomorrow morning and go back to the settlement."

"I suppose that makes sense," Eden said. "There's still so much that they have to figure out and with everything that we found out when we were on the settlement, and then even more when we talked to Creia, uniting the species and piecing the planet back together is going to take time and effort. Besides, I don't blame Rain at all for not wanting to go back to Earth."

"You don't?" Pyra asked.

"Of course not. What does she have there? She left so long ago that she wouldn't even be able to recognize it now. Everyone who she has ever known and loved is dead now and she doesn't have a home or a career or anything to go back to. She has a home here, and Lynx. Going back to Earth would just be a reminder of everything that she's lost and would put her right in the spotlight, which I know that I wouldn't want. Her life is here now."

"Is your life here now?" Pyra asked.

Eden folded another blanket and looked over her shoulder at him.

"Of course it is," she said. "Why would you even ask that?"

"I was just wondering if you ever thought about moving back to Earth. You left everything behind there without thinking that you wouldn't ever go back. You left all of those things that you said that Rain doesn't have to go back to; your home, your career, your friends. Do you ever wish that you were back there?"

"I don't wish that I was there, Pyra. There are times when I miss things that are there, but not enough that I would ever want to leave what I have here. Uoria is my home now. I feel more settled and comfortable here among the Denynso than I ever did when I was living on Earth. I want to be a part of everything that is happening here. Just think about it. I came here thinking that I was going to be on one small compound for no more than six months. I was going to do a little bit of studying, do some research, and then go back to Ryan hoping that somewhere along the way I could come up with an excuse as to why I didn't have any warrior blood to give him."

"So you never actually intended on trying to get blood from one of us for him?"

"No. I think I told myself that I did, that I was going to be the courageous scientific pioneer who helped make some of the most groundbreaking discoveries and advancements of our time by braving the fierce Denynso and coming away with my life and some blood." Pyra gave a short laugh and Eden grinned at him. "But when it came right down to it, I knew that I couldn't do that. Not only was it so incredibly stupidly dangerous that it would have essentially been suicide, which, of course, Ryan knew the whole time which is why he decided to force me to do it in the first place, but I also had a really terrible feeling from the first moment that he told me that he wanted to do experiments with Denynso blood."

"What kind of terrible feeling?"

Eden folded the last blanket and tucked the stacks of blankets and clothes back into the basket so that she could put it on the floor beside Lysander's cradle. She sighed, trying to come up with the right words to explain to Pyra what she had been thinking and feeling when Ryan first started talking about his plans for experimenting with the highly sought-after, and highly illegal, blood of the Denynso warriors.

"I worked with Ryan for a long time. It gave me a chance to really get to know him, both inside the lab and out, and he was not the person that everybody thought he was."

"I know. You told me about the things that he did to you, or at least tried to do to you."

"It's more than that," Eden said, walking over to Pyra and resting her hand briefly on the back of her baby son's head. "I think that people underestimate him. They think that he is a bit eccentric, but I think that it is something much darker than that. I think that he is capable of far more than anyone has imagined."

TBC

(To be continued in book II...)

www.ingramcontent.com/pod-product-compliance
Lightning Source LLC
Chambersburg PA
CBHW032044180726
48284CB00008B/2751